Winnie the Pooh's
Rainy-Day
Activities

By Sharee Hopler
Crafts photography by Brian Stanton

Disney PRESS

New York

For Nancy, who helped make it
possible for children to play safely

Copyright © 2002 Disney Enterprises, Inc.

Text and illustrations for *Winnie the Pooh and the Honey Tree* © 1993 Disney Press.
Text and illustrations for *Winnie the Pooh and the Blustery Day* © 1993 Disney Press.
Text and illustrations for *Winnie the Pooh and Tigger, Too* © 1994 Disney Press.
Text and illustrations for *Winnie the Pooh and a Day for Eeyore* © 1994 Disney Press.
Text and illustrations for "It Was There … Now It's Gone," "Rabbit's Rules," and "I Bounce" from *Lessons from the Hundred-Acre Wood* © 1999 Disney Press.
Text and illustrations for "Piglet Shows Some Talent" from *Oh Bother! Pooh's Book About Trying New Things* © 2001 Disney Press.

Based on the "Winnie the Pooh" works by A. A. Milne and E. H. Shepard

First Edition
10 9 8 7 6 5 4 3 2 1
Library of Congress Catalog Card Number: 2001095758
ISBN 0-7868-3366-1

Visit www.disneybooks.com

Page 38

Craft
Table of Contents

Page 62

Page 6

Page 22

Page 10

From *Winnie the Pooh and the Honey Tree* . . .

"You can't get honey with a balloon," Christopher Robin told Pooh.

"*I* can," said Pooh. "I shall hang on to the string and float up to the bee hole."

Then Pooh rolled himself in mud until he was covered from his nose to his toes.

"I'm pretending to be a little black storm cloud," Pooh said, "to fool the bees."

"Silly old bear," said Christopher Robin. He watched Pooh float up, up, up and dangle right beside the hole.

Pooh reached in and pulled out a pawful of golden honey as the bees began to buzz suspiciously around his head.

"Christopher Robin!" called Pooh. "I think the bees suspect that I am not a little black storm cloud!"

With a swoosh, the balloon's string loosened, and the balloon began to lose air. It swooshed all around, with Pooh trailing along for the ride.

Then the balloon had no more air at all, and down Pooh went, landing right on top of Christopher Robin!

"Oh dear," said Pooh, "I guess it all comes from liking honey so much!"

Pooh's Honeybee Shaker

Buzz, buzz, buzz.
Pooh knows that where there are bees, there's usually honey. The bees in this shaker can make quiet, humming buzzes or loud, angry, "leave our honey alone, please" buzzes, depending on how hard you shake them.

Apparently, bees have more brain than one would think.

Here's What You Need:

- 2 clear plastic cups
- 9-10 round wooden beads (approximately ¾" in diameter)
- Yellow and black electrical tape
- Wooden skewers
- Yellow acrylic paint
- Paintbrush
- Bowl
- Masking tape
- Scissors

Here's What You Do:

1 Thread beads onto skewer and place across bowl. Tape down ends of skewer with masking tape to hold in place while you paint the beads.

2 Paint the beads with yellow acrylic paint and let dry completely.

3 Cut thin strips from the black electrical tape and tape around the beads to make the bees' stripes.

4 Place the finished bees inside the cups and, using the yellow and black electrical tape, tape the cups together.

From *Winnie the Pooh and the Blustery Day . . .*

On this blustery day, Piglet had just swept away the last leaf when a gust of wind blew it right back at him, scooping him up and whisking him away. He blew right by Pooh, who grabbed hold of Piglet's scarf just before Piglet floated out of reach.

"Oh Pooh, I'm unraveling!" Piglet cried. Indeed he was. Or, rather, his scarf was.

Piglet went sailing off into the sky with Pooh in tow on the ground.

"Oh dear, oh-dear-oh-dear!" cried Piglet as he swooped right and left in the gusty air.

"Oh bo-bo-bother!" Pooh exclaimed.

When Piglet finally looked down, there was Eeyore busy repairing his

house, which the wind had blown to pieces. He had just put the last stick back in place when Pooh came crashing through.

"Happy Windsday, Eeyore," said Pooh. Then he went zipping off again, still holding on to the remains of Piglet's scarf.

"Thanks for noticin' me," said Eeyore.

Eeyore's Home, Sweet Home

Every once in a while, after an especially windy day or an especially bouncy Tigger, one's house needs to be rebuilt.

Here's What You Need:

- Sticks and twigs of various sizes* (approximately 6"-7" in length)
- Double-sided tape
- Moss (optional)
- Craft glue
- 3 squares (6"x 6" each) of thick cardboard
- Masking tape

Here's What You Do:

1 Using the masking tape, tape the cardboard squares together to form a triangle.

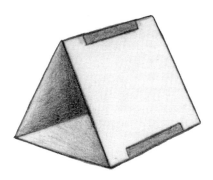

2 Place strips of double-sided tape horizontally along the sides of the hut.

3 Lean thicker sticks and twigs vertically against the sides and press firmly to secure. Fill in the gaps with thinner twigs, pressing firmly against the tape.

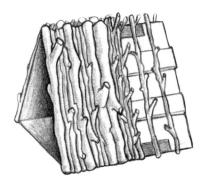

4 If there are still bare spots, attach more twigs to your sturdy foundation with glue.

5 If you like, you may place moss inside the hut to give Eeyore a soft spot to sit. He'll be so pleased.

* If you haven't access to twigs, cinnamon sticks will work just splendidly. Craft stores carry cinnamon sticks that are the perfect length for Eeyore's house.

From *Piglet Shows Some Talent . . .*

Owl was in the middle of a story. "My great-great-grand-great-uncle, the famous thespian—"

"The what?" Piglet whispered to Pooh.

Pooh had no idea, so it was lucky that Owl overheard. "A thespian is an actor," Owl explained, "one who makes a living on the stage. So many speeches, such talent. More cake?"

"Please," said Pooh, though he'd had plenty.

"No one performed the dance of the fifty feathers as well as my dear uncle," Owl said. "The audience

loved the show. Everyone loved my uncle."

All of a sudden, Owl came up with an idea. "Let's have a talent show!" he said. "Everyone can do something. I will, of course, offer my services as director."

"Sounds fun," Pooh agreed.

"But what will *I* do?" Piglet asked. "Oh d-d-dear."

"Now, now," Owl told him, "I'll teach you the dance of the fifty feathers. You'll catch on in no time."

The next day, Owl tried to teach Piglet the dance of the fifty feathers. But Piglet could barely manage with two.

"It's just as well," Pooh told his friend. "It was hard enough to find those two feathers. Where would we get fifty?"

Owl's Feathers—A Card Game

It's no wonder Piglet couldn't find any feathers—you've got them all! Put them to good use with this fun matching game.

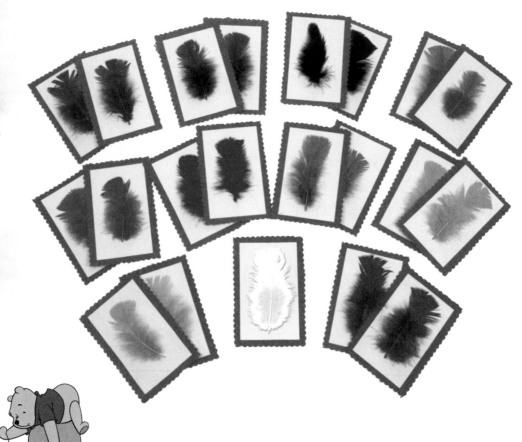

Here's What You Need:

- Scissors
- 21 unlined, 3" x 5" index cards
- 1 bag of colorful feathers (available at craft stores)
- Double-sided tape
- 6 sheets of 9" x 12" construction paper (any color)
- Scallop-edged scissors (available at craft stores)
- Glue stick

Here's What You Do:

1 Choose two feathers of each color and set aside ten pairs. Select one white feather.

2 Apply length of double-sided tape to each unlined index card and, pressing firmly, secure all twenty-one feathers onto the cards, one per card.

3 Cut the construction paper sheets into four equal rectangles, making twenty-four in all. Using a glue stick, glue one feathered index card to each construction paper rectangle. Discard unused rectangles.

4 Trim construction paper with scallop-edged scissors to make a decorative edge.

The game proceeds thusly:

Deal all the Owl's Feathers cards, feather side down, in equal piles. Each player picks up his/her cards, makes matches with the same colored feathers, and places them faceup on the table.

Moving clockwise from the dealer, players take turns selecting cards from one another's hands. When you have a match, place it faceup on the table. Once all pairs are matched, there will be one player left with the white feather card. Congratulations! The player with the white feather card gets to go first the next time the game is played.

I Bounce

Oh, if you could only know
How it feels to go and

Bounce and bounce and bounce—

To leave the earth
For a moment or so and

Bounce and bounce and bounce.

I bounce into sky—
Endlessly blue!
I bounce so high—
I FLY from this world
For a moment or two and I—
Bounce and bounce and bounce!

Tigger Tail Necklace

Wearing your Tigger Tail Necklace will help make the world a bouncier place! (And don't be surprised if you're a bit boingier, too!)

Here's What You Need:

- Pipe cleaners
- Cheerios (or other holey cereal)
- Black cord
- Scissors
- Pencil or crayon
- Needle-nosed pliers

Here's What You Do:

Pipe Cleaner Preparation

Grown-ups only, please: cut pipe cleaners in half. With pliers, fold back each pipe cleaner approximately 1/4" from the ends so the sharp ends become nicely rounded.

Now we're ready to begin:

1 Wrap one of the pieces of pipe cleaner around the pencil—making coils close together for tight tails, farther apart for loose ones.

2 Slide the tail off the pencil and flip up the first coil to form a loop.

3 Thread tail loops onto cord, alternating Tigger tails with cereal pieces.

Bouncing is what tiggers do best. Hoo-hoo-hoo!

From *Winnie the Pooh and the Honey Tree . . .*

Rabbit sat at the table and watched Pooh eat. Pooh ate and ate until there was no more honey left in Rabbit's house. At last, he rose from the table and said, "Good-bye, Rabbit, I must be going." And he started out Rabbit's front door.

Pooh's head reached the outdoors and his feet dangled indoors, but his middle got stuck in the middle! Pooh tried to go out. He couldn't. He tried to go in. But he couldn't do that, either. "Oh bother!" said Pooh. "It all comes from not having a big enough front door."

"Nonsense!" said Rabbit sharply. "It all comes from eating too much!" And he hurried out his back door to fetch some help.

Now there was nothing for Pooh to do but wait. He looked at the trees blowing in the breeze. He watched the clouds sailing by in the blue sky.

More time passed, and still Pooh wasn't getting any thinner.

Kanga brought Roo for a visit. "I brought you some honeysuckle, Pooh," said Roo.

"*Honey*suckle?" asked Pooh hungrily.

"No, Pooh," said Kanga, laughing. "You don't eat it—you smell it."

Pooh buried his nose in the flowers and sniffed.

Kanga and Roo's Honeysuckle Bouquet

Kanga and Roo visit Pooh with a honeysuckle bouquet to cheer him up in his time of great tightness. But remember— no matter how delicious they smell, these sweet blossoms are not for eating!

Here's What You Need:

- Approximately 30 foil and 30 plain mini-cupcake liners
- Approximately 15 green pipe cleaners
- Colored raffia

Here's What You Do:

1 Flatten out the liners to make small round circles.

2 To make a flower, bend a pipe cleaner in half. Scrunch a white cupcake liner together at its middle and place it in the fold of the pipe cleaner. Twist one half of the pipe cleaner around the other to secure the cupcake liner (flower) to the stem.

3 Twist pipe cleaner again and add another flower by placing a scrunched foil cupcake liner between the two halves of the pipe cleaner. Twist the two halves of the pipe cleaner together to secure. Repeat, adding another white flower and another foil one.

4 Continue to twist the two pipe-cleaner halves together to make a stem. If you wish, about halfway down the stem add a leaf by looping one half of the pipe cleaner out and back around the other half. Finish twisting until there are no more ends left to twist.

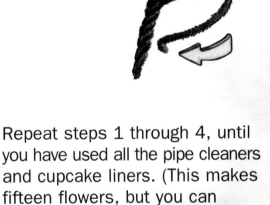

5 Repeat steps 1 through 4, until you have used all the pipe cleaners and cupcake liners. (This makes fifteen flowers, but you can create as many as you like!)

Fluff flowers and place in a vase, or tie stems together with colorful raffia, and give to someone you know. (A spritz or two of perfume or cologne will make your bouquet smell delicious.)

From *Winnie the Pooh and a Day for Eeyore* . . .

A big brown pinecone dropped—*PLOP!*—right on Pooh's head. He picked it up and gazed at it thoughtfully. As he walked along, he decided to make up a little poem. But while his head was occupied, his feet tripped over a tree root, and Pooh tumbled to the ground.

Pooh kept on tumbling until he came to a stop on the bridge, just as the pinecone went skittering over the edge and into the water below.

"That's funny," Pooh said to himself, as the pinecone drifted under the bridge. "I dropped it on one side, and it came out on the other. I wonder if it would do that again."

So he collected a rather large pinecone and a rather small one and tossed them over the far side of the bridge. Then he scurried to the other side and waited.

"I wonder which one will come out first," said Pooh.

Well, as it turned out, the big one came out first, and the little one came out last, which was just what Pooh had hoped. And that was the beginning of a game called Pooh Sticks, named for its inventor— Winnie the Pooh.

Now, you might think it should have been called Pooh *Cones*, but since it was easier to collect a handful of sticks than an armful of cones, Pooh made a slight improvement on his original game.

Pooh's Stones-
and-Cones Game

It's funny how a good idea can actually drop out of
the sky, which is exactly what happened to Pooh
and how the game of Pooh Sticks came to be.

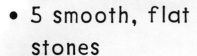

Here's What You Need:

- 5 smooth, flat stones
- Colored electrical tape—red, blue, green, white, and yellow

- 5 pinecones
- Scissors
- 12" x 12" square of red felt
- Paint (optional)
- Sheet of stick-on letters (optional)

Here's What You Do:

1 Make a grid on the felt square in a tic-tac-toe, game-board pattern, using the electrical tape.

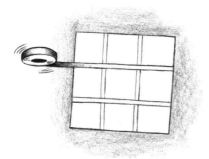

2 Border edges with tape.

3 If you like, decorate your stones with paint or stick-on letters.

Now you've got yourself a completely portable tic-tac-toe game board that you can take with you wherever you go. If you can't find pinecones and stones, you've still got a game! Just use two different groups of objects—sugar packets and toothpicks, for example.

It Was There . . .
Now It's Gone

You think you can depend on **tails**.

You don't expect **tails** to go wrong.

The last time I looked, it was right there.

Now when I look there,

it's gone!

It was always just behind me,

Always tagging along.

A little something at the back . . .

I thought it was there—and **it's gone**.

I assumed it was attached to me,

That it actually hung true.

I'd hoped it was stuck very firmly on.

Maybe we needed some glue.

It used to trail right behind me,

Always tailing along.

My little extra at the back . . .

I thought it was there—now **it's gone**.

Eeyore's Tail Money Sock

Gloomy ol' Eeyore is always losing his tail. As he says, "You never know with a tail!" But sooner or later, someone always finds it! Pin your very own Eeyore tail to the wall of your bedroom, and it will hold all your spare change. Be careful not to lose it!

Here's What You Need:

- Craft knife (grown-ups only)
- 1 gray tube sock (no heel)
- Adhesive-backed black felt (approximately 9"x12")
- Scissors
- 1 yard of pink ribbon (approximately 2" wide)
- Sheet of tracing paper
- Pencil
- Pushpin
- 1 large black button
- Craft glue

Here's What You Do:

1 Using a pencil, trace tail pattern (from page 64) onto sheet of tracing paper and cut out. Trace tail cutout onto paper backing of the adhesive-backed felt and cut out the shape.

2 **Grown-ups only, please:** with a craft knife, cut a large V in the paper backing of the felt. Remove only the V-shaped paper from the adhesive backing.

3 Pressing firmly, attach the felt cutout to the toe end of the sock.

4 With pink ribbon, tie a bow loosely above the felt tail end, gathering the sock together just a bit, but leaving enough space for change to fall into the toe of the sock.

5 Glue the button to the head of the pushpin, using craft glue. Let dry completely.

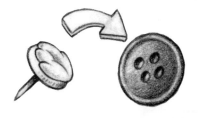

6 Push the pushpin through the sock cuff and hang from a wall or door frame. Voilà! You're ready to start saving for another rainy day.

From *Winnie the Pooh and the Honey Tree* . . .

"Hello, Pooh," said Owl. "Are you stuck?"

"Oh no!" said Pooh. "I'm just resting."

"Pooh," said Owl, "you are definitely stuck. You are a wedged bear in a great tightness. This situation calls for an expert!"

"Did someone say 'expert'?" asked Gopher. "Gopher's my name–digging's my game. Now, what seems to be the problem?"

Gopher quickly inspected the situation. "The problem with this door," he said, "is that it has a bear in it. Now we could dig him out, or we could dynamite him out."

"Dynamite?" Pooh said in a very small voice.

"Dynamite!" exclaimed Owl. "Nonsense! We can't dynamite. We might hurt him!"

"Well, think it over," said Gopher.

Gopher's "Dynamite" Mining Helmet

Gopher is always "popping up" with well-intentioned suggestions that usually involve dynamite. You can create this helmet to go on a digging expedition of your own.

Here's What You Need:

- Scissors
- 4 sheets of newspaper
- Masking tape
- 2 mixing bowls (each about 6" and 7" in diameter)
- Toilet-paper tube
- Gesso paint (available at craft stores)
- Yellow acrylic craft paint
- Paintbrush
- 1 craft foam ball approximately 2½" in diameter (cut in half by a grown-up)
- Aluminum foil
- Rubber band

Here's What You Do:

1 Place the four newspaper sheets over the top—and slightly off center—of the larger mixing bowl.

2 Using the smaller mixing bowl, press the newspaper firmly down inside the larger bowl.

3 Remove the smaller bowl, and using the masking tape liberally (which will not only give your helmet a strong foundation but is good for one's sense of well-being), tape the entire top surface of the newspaper over and over and over again. When you're tired of taping, you're done.

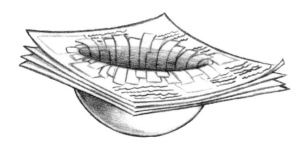

4 Now fold the overhanging newspaper edges into the bowl and tape down, leaving the portion of overhang that is longer than the rest. This will become the visor of your mining helmet.

5 Sculpt the shape of the visor by folding and using more masking tape.

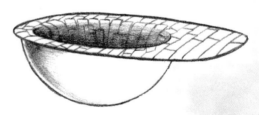

6 Cut an approximately 2″ segment from the end of the toilet-paper roll.

7 Tape the 2″ segment to the front of the helmet just above the visor.

8 Paint helmet with Gesso and let dry.

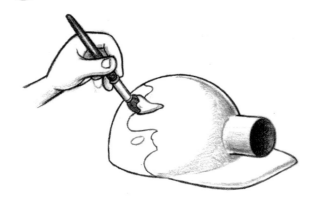

9 Paint helmet with yellow paint and let dry.

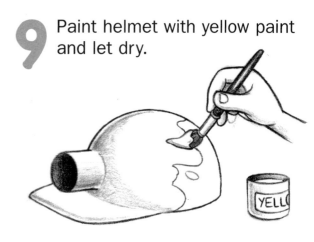

10 Place craft foam in center of aluminum square, flat side down, and gather together edges of foil to cover. Twist excess foil to form stem end of the lightbulb, and secure with a rubber band.

11 "Screw" lightbulb into light socket. Lights on, everyone— we're off for some excavatin'!

Rabbit's Rules

1. No bouncing.

2. Don't eat so much at lunchtime that you get stuck in my doorway.

3. Don't talk while I'm thinking.

4. Keep out of my garden.

5. No bouncing in my garden.

6. Absolutely no bouncing allowed.

7. This means you!!!

Thank you for your cooperation.

Ol' Long Ears Headband

Tigger saves his biggest bounces for his good friend Rabbit, who, truth be told, would rather not be bounced at all. You'll look a lot like Ol' Long Ears himself with these ears, so you'll want to be on the look-out for a tigger in need of bouncing someone.

Here's What You Need:

- Pencil
- Tracing paper
- Scissors
- Pink construction paper
- 2 paper clips
- Headband
- Yellow crepe paper
- Clear tape
- Yellow poster board
- Glue stick

Here's What You Do:

1 Wrap crepe paper around the headband until the headband is totally covered. Secure ends with clear tape.

2 Trace two rabbit-shaped ears with 2" extensions (pattern found on page 65) onto tracing paper and cut out. Trace cutout pattern onto the poster board and cut out.

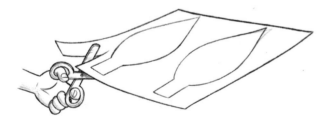

3 Trace two inner-ear shapes (pattern found on page 65) onto tracing paper and cut out. Trace cutout pattern onto pink construction paper and cut out.

4 Glue pink ear shapes onto yellow outer-ear shapes.

5 Unfold paper clip halfway into an L shape and tape shorter part of the L crosswise to the headband.

6 Tape the ears to the longer part of the paper clip and wrap the 2" extensions around the headband, gluing back to front. Tape securely. Now don't be surprised if someone rushes up and begins to introduce himself with a T-I-double-Guh-Rrr.

From *Winnie the Pooh and a Day for Eeyore . . .*

Piglet was running along with a big red balloon when he accidentally ran smack into a tree. He bounced off the tree and came to a stop—*POP!*— right on top of what *had been* the big red balloon.

"Oh d-d-dear. Well . . . maybe Eeyore doesn't like balloons so very much," Piglet said.

So he went off to see Eeyore, dragging the remains of the balloon behind him.

"Many happy returns of the day!" Piglet sang out when he saw Eeyore.

"Meaning my birthday," Eeyore said glumly.

"Yes," said Piglet. "And I've brought you a balloon but I'm afraid, I'm very sorry, but . . ."

Eeyore took one look at what was left of his birthday balloon and said, "Red. My favorite color."

Just then Pooh appeared. "I've brought you a little present, Eyore," he announced. "It's a useful pot to put things in."

"Like a balloon?" Eeyore said hopefully.

"Oh no. Balloons are much too big. . . ." Pooh began, as Eeyore picked up the balloon with his teeth and dropped it into the very useful pot.

"It *does* fit!" Pooh marveled. "Eeyore, I'm very glad I thought of giving you a useful pot to put things in."

"And I'm very glad I thought of giving you something to put in a useful pot," said Piglet.

Eeyore didn't say anything. But he looked very, very glad.

Eeyore's Birthday Balloon Wrapping Paper

As Piglet can tell you, balloons come in two varieties—those with air and those without. You can make a balloon-shaped stamp and create a very special wrapping paper.

Here's What You Need:

- Masking tape
- 1 potato
- Sharp knife (grown-ups only)
- Plastic plate
- 1 roll of kraft paper
- Black marker
- Sponge
- Red craft paint

Here's What You Do:

1 Unroll paper and tape down edges with masking tape so you have a smooth, flat working surface.

2 **Grown-ups only, please:** cut potato in half crosswise at roundest part to make balloon shape.

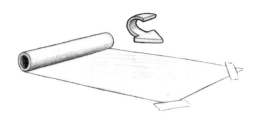

3 Pour red paint onto plastic plate.

4 Stamp potato in paint and dab excess onto sponge.

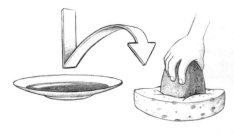

5 Press potato firmly onto paper in random designs or in patterns. Let dry completely.

6 Using the black marker, give each of your balloons a string. This is so they will not float off the paper, leaving you with an empty sort of wrapping paper and a third variety of balloon—one that isn't there anymore.

43

From *Winnie the Pooh and Tigger, Too . . .*

"There, that should do it," said Rabbit as he gathered up an armload of carrots from his garden. But then he heard a sound he knew all too well: *BOING! BOING! BOING!*

"Oh no!" cried Rabbit. "Stop!"

But Tigger didn't stop. He bounced Rabbit right off his feet, sending the carrots flying every which way.

"Hello, Rabbit! It's me, Tigger," said Tigger. "That's T-I-double-Guh-Rrr...."

"Oh please, please! Don't spell it," moaned Rabbit, sitting up and pushing Tigger away. "Oh Tigger, won't you ever stop bouncing?"

Rabbit's Garden Apron

Oh no! It's happened again. Tigger's dropped by, and Rabbit's newly gathered carrots are flying out of *his* arms and on to *your* apron.

Here's What You Need:

- Plain, child-sized apron
- Fabric crayons— orange, green, and dark purple
- Sheet of nonglossy drawing paper
- 2-3 sheets of unprinted white paper
- Iron and ironing board
- Newspaper sheets

Here's What You Do:

1 With fabric crayons, draw carrots all over the sheet of drawing paper. The more pressure you apply, the brighter the color will be.

2 Place items in the following order on the ironing board: first, one or two plain sheets of paper; then, several layers of newspaper; and finally, a sheet of unprinted white paper. Place apron (faceup) on top. Lay paper design facedown on fabric. Place a clean sheet of paper between iron and paper design.

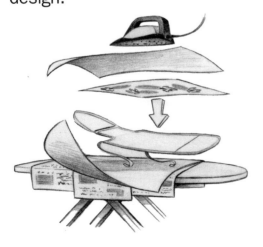

3 **Grown-ups only, please:** using a cotton setting (no steam), iron with steady pressure over entire surface of paper design until image becomes slightly visible through paper. Lift iron when moving from place to place, to avoid smudging the carrots.

4 Remove design paper carefully.

Note: when your apron needs cleaning, machine-wash, using warm water and gentle action. Do not use bleach or place in dryer.

Wear your apron the next time you cook or craft, and you'll stay neat and tidy— just like Rabbit!

From *Winnie the Pooh and the Blustery Day* . . .

As soon as the flood was over, Christopher Robin threw Pooh a hero party for rescuing Piglet. Pooh's hero party had barely begun when Eeyore arrived.

"I found a house for Owl," he said. "Follow me."

So everyone followed Eeyore. But much to their surprise, when they got to Owl's new house, it turned out to be . . . Piglet's house!

"This is Owl's new house," Eeyore said proudly.

"It's a nice house, Eeyore," Christopher Robin said, "but ..."

"It's the best house in the whole world," Piglet said with a sigh. Piglet didn't have the heart to disappoint Owl. He had lost his house in the flood, after all.

"But Piglet," Rabbit said, "where will you live?"

"With me," Pooh said.

"With you?" Piglet said, wiping a tear from his eye. "Oh thank you, Pooh Bear. Of course I will."

"Piglet, that was a very heroic thing to do," Christopher Robin said.

"Let's make a one-hero party into a two-hero party!" suggested Pooh.

Pooh was a hero for saving Piglet, and Piglet was a hero for giving Owl his home.

Then Pooh and Piglet were scooped up in a blanket and tossed high, into the clear, blue sky.

Piglet's Hero Trophy

Even the smallest act of bravery is worthy of recognition. Be sure to have a sizable trophy on hand for just such an occasion.

Here's What You Need:

- Wooden pieces of various shapes and sizes (available at craft stores)
- 1 or 2 CD cases
- Craft glue
- Assorted flat-backed jewels (available at craft stores)
- Sheet of stick-on letters

Here's What You Do:

1 Spread your wood pieces, jewels, and sticker sheet out on a table.

2 Start designing your own hero trophy, or follow the one in the picture!

3 Experiment before you start gluing. Your trophy can be wide and low or tall and spindly. Use a CD case as a base (or two cases for a three-level trophy).

4 Assemble your trophy! Once the glue has dried, decorate your trophy with sparkly jewels and stick-on letters.

Now, since you've got a trophy and a card game, why not have a hero party? It's just the thing to celebrate braveries large and small. Here are some ideas for your hero party:

- Blanket toss-up of some of your favorite stuffed animals

- Rousing game of Owl's Feathers

- Refreshments, especially a smackeral of honey for your guests

- Hero parade, complete with drum (pot and wooden spoon), shaker (a container of loud honeybees would do nicely), and trumpet (paper-towel roll)

- Trophy presentation, with lots of handshakes and hugs all around

From *Winnie the Pooh and the Honey Tree* . . .

Rabbit soon grew tired of seeing Pooh's bottom and legs where his front door used to be, so he wedged a picture frame around Pooh and put a lace doily on Pooh's bottom. "And now for a little dash of color," he said, and set a flowerpot on top of the doily on top of Pooh. But Pooh kicked his legs, and the flowerpot went crashing to the ground.

Next, Rabbit found two branches that looked
like antlers. With a paintbrush, he painted a moose
face right on Pooh's bottom.

For a finishing touch, Rabbit found a board and
put it across Pooh's legs like a shelf. "Now that's
more like it!" he said.

Rabbit's Wall Hanging

Sometimes when there's a bear wedged snugly in your front door, the only sensible thing to do is to decorate him.

Here's What You Need:

- Yellow modeling clay (lightweight and air-drying)
- 2 antler-shaped twigs approximately 2"- 3" long
- Permanent black marker
- 12" embroidery hoop
- 14" x 14" fabric square
- Scissors
- Craft glue

54

Here's What You Do:

1 Work the modeling clay into a rather large ball (one that resembles a bear's behind) and press against tabletop to flatten on one side.

2 Press ends of twigs into clay for the antlers and set aside to harden.

3 Place fabric in embroidery hoop and trim edges within 1" of the hoop.

4 When bear's behind is completely dry, draw on a face with permanent black marker.

5 Center bear's behind within framed fabric and attach, using craft glue.

6 When it's completely dry, hang your wall decoration from the ring at the top of the embroidery hoop.

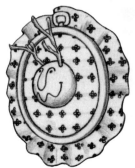

From *Winnie the Pooh and Tigger, Too . . .*

One fine day in the Hundred-Acre Wood, Winnie the Pooh was sitting on a comfortable log in his Thoughtful Spot when his thoughts were interrupted by a sound he knew very well: *BOING! BOING! BOING!*

"Hello, Pooh! It's me, Tigger!" exclaimed Tigger, bounding into the Thoughtful Spot and bouncing Pooh right off his log. "T-I-double-Guh-Rrr spells Tigger!"

"Yes, I know," said Pooh. "You've bounced me before."

Tigger jumped up and shook Pooh's hand. "Well, I'd better be going now. I have a lot more bouncing to do."

Nearby, Piglet was busy sweeping up outside his house. He began to hear a noise, which started off smaller than Piglet himself but grew larger and larger. Suddenly, the noise turned into Tigger, who bounced Piglet right off his feet.

"Ooh, Tigger. You scared me!" said Piglet.

"I did? But I gave you one of my littlest bounces. I'm saving my biggest one for Ol' Long Ears," Tigger said. He pulled up his ears as far as they would go, trying to look like Rabbit.

"Well, I'm glad I got one of your little bounces. Thank you, Tigger," said Piglet. He waved good-bye as Tigger bounced off down the road. *BOING! BOING! BOING!*

Torn-Paper Tigger Collage

This is an activity to be attacked with wild abandon; think of yourself as a tigger and go!

Here's What You Need:

- Construction paper—white, brown, orange, purple, and black
- Larger-sized black paper for mounting
- Glue stick
- Scissors

Here's What You Do:

1 Tear paper into shapes: strips for stripes; ovals for body, arms, and legs; circles for a nose; and irregular shapes for head and tail.

2 Arrange the pieces into a tigger shape, and glue onto white paper.

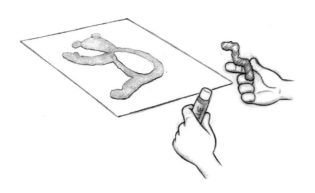

3 Cut triangles into the edges of the white paper.

4 Glue white paper onto black mounting paper. If you have other colors, you can make a complete gallery of Hundred-Acre friends: yellow, red, and black for Pooh; black and light and dark pink for Piglet; pink, black, and light and dark gray for Eeyore; yellow, pink, and black for Rabbit; brown, black, blue, and pink for Kanga and Roo; and brown, yellow, pink, and black for Owl.

If done correctly, after you finish your collage, you should be left with a good-sized pile of paper scraps. Hmm . . . now what would a tigger do with a lovely pile of paper scraps? Why, he'd bounce them, of course. Hoo-hoo-hoo!

From *Winnie the Pooh and a Day for Eeyore* . . .

"What are you giving Eeyore for his birthday?" Pooh asked Owl.

"I, ah . . . Well, what are *you* giving him, Pooh?" Owl asked.

"I'm giving him this useful pot to keep things in," said Pooh, holding out an empty honeypot.

"A useful pot?" said Owl, peering into the jar. "Evidently, someone has been keeping honey in it."

"Yes," said Pooh. "It's very useful like that, but I wanted to ask you—"

"You ought to write 'Happy Birthday' on it," said Owl.

"That was what I wanted to ask you," explained Pooh. "My own spelling is a bit wobbly."

"Very well," Owl said. And he took the pot and his

pen and got down to work. "It's easier if people don't look while I'm writing," he added, turning his back on Pooh.

After what seemed a rather long time, Owl turned around again. "There!" he said, proudly holding up the pot. "All finished. What do you think of it?"

"It looks like a lot of words just to say 'Happy Birthday,'" Pooh pointed out.

"Well, actually, I wrote, 'A Very Happy Birthday, with Love from Pooh,'" Owl explained. "Naturally, it takes a good deal of words to say something like that."

"Oh I see," Pooh said, taking the pot. "Thank you, Owl."

A Useful Pot to Put Things In

One can never have too many useful pots to put things in, don't you think? This one would come in very handy for holding your Pooh Stones-and-Cones.

Here's What You Need:

- Terra-cotta pot
- Acrylic craft paint—color(s) of your choice
- Paintbrush
- Black permanent marker

Here's What You Do:

1 Paint your pot in whatever colors tickle your fancy. Let dry completely.

2 Decorate with pictures and/or words. Owl wrote, "Hipy Papy Bthuthdth Thu Hda Bthuthdy" ("A Very Happy Birthday with Love from Pooh") on the useful pot Pooh gave to Eeyore.

A Hum from Pooh Bear

Crafting with you is a whole lot of fun.

Just thinking about all the things we have done

Makes me feel happy inside and out.

I guess that's what being friends is about.

See **Eeyore's Tail Money Sock**
page 30

Eeyore's Tail

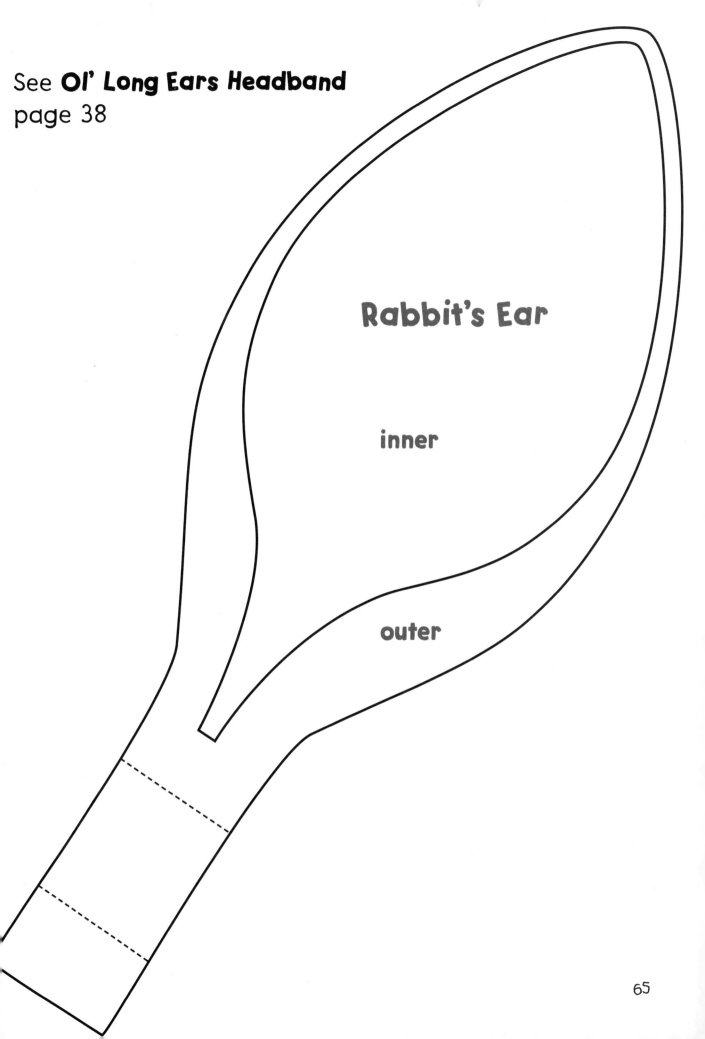

See **Ol' Long Ears Headband**
page 38

Rabbit's Ear

inner

outer